Gymnastics

A Level Two Reader

By Cynthia Klingel

Gymnastics is a beautiful sport to watch. A gymnast is strong and limber.

Do you want to be a gymnast? It takes a lot of practice. Gymnasts practice in special gyms.

There are different pieces of equipment to use. Girls perform on the uneven bars, the vault, the balance beam, and the floor.

Boys use the parallel bars, the horizontal bar, the pommel horse, the rings, the vault, and the floor.

Before doing gymnastics, it is important to warm up. It helps keep the gymnasts from hurting themselves.

Gymnasts use their bodies to make different shapes. They do different poses to show their balance.

13

Gymnasts learn tumbling skills. Two beginning skills are forward and backward rolls. Two more are headstands and handstands.

Gymnasts also learn jumps and leaps. Some gymnasts leap so well, it looks like flying!

After learning these skills, you can put them together. Now you have a gymnastics routine to perform with music.

You have worked hard.

You are gymnasts!

Index

To Find Out More

Books

Bailer, Darice. *Solid Gold: Gymnastic Stars.* New York: Random House, 2000.

Bizley, Kirk. *Gymnastics.* Chicago: Heinemann Library, 1999.

Feldman, Jane. *I Love Gymnastics!* New York: Random House, Inc., 2000.

Kalman, Bobbie, and Tammy Everts. *Gymnastics.* New York: Crabtree Publishing Company, 1997.

Web Sites

Visit our homepage for lots of links about gymnastics:
http://www.childsworld.com/links.html

Note to Parents, Teachers, and Librarians:
We routinely verify our Web links to make sure they're safe, active sites—so encourage your readers to check them out!

Note to Parents and Educators

Welcome to Wonder Books®! These books provide text at three different levels for beginning readers to practice and strengthen their reading skills. Additionally, the use of nonfiction text provides readers the valuable opportunity to *read to learn*, not just to learn to read.

These leveled readers allow children to choose books at their level of reading confidence and performance. Nonfiction Level One books offer beginning readers simple language, word choice, and sentence structure as well as a word list. Nonfiction Level Two books feature slightly more difficult vocabulary, longer sentences, and longer total text. In the back of each Nonfiction Level Two book are an index and a list of books and Web sites for finding out more information. Nonfiction Level Three books continue to extend word choice and length of text. In the back of each Nonfiction Level Three book are a glossary, an index, and a list of books and Web sites for further research.

State and national standards in reading and language arts emphasize using nonfiction at all levels of reading development. Wonder Books® fill the historical void in nonfiction material for primary grade readers with the additional benefit of a leveled text.

About the Author

Cynthia Klingel has worked as a high school English teacher and an elementary school teacher. She is currently the curriculum director for a Minnesota school district. Cynthia lives with her family in Mankato, Minnesota.

Readers should remember...
All sports carry a certain amount of risk. To reduce the risk of injury while doing gymnastics, perform at your own level and use care and common sense. The publisher and author take no responsibility or liability for injuries resulting from doing gymnastics.

Published by The Child's World®
P.O. Box 326
Chanhassen, MN 55317-0326
800-599-READ
www.childsworld.com

Photo Credits
© David Turnley/CORBIS:10
© Jennie Woodcock/CORBIS: 6
© Jim Cummins/Taxi/GettyImages: cover, 5, 17
© MugShots/CORBIS: 18
© PhotoEdit: 21
© Spencer Grant/PhotoEdit: 14
© Terje Rakke/The ImageBank: 2
© Tony Freeman/PhotoEdit: 13
© William Sallaz/CORBIS: 9

Editorial Directions, Inc.: E. Russell Primm and Emily J. Dolbear, Editors;
Flanagan Publishing Services, Photo Researcher

The Child's World®: Mary Berendes, Publishing Director

Library of Congress Cataloging-in-Publication Data
Klingel, Cynthia Fitterer.
  Gymnastics / by Cynthia Klingel.
    p. cm. — (Wonder books)
"A Level Two Reader."
Summary: Simple text describes the sport of gymnastics and how certain stunts are performed.
Includes bibliographical references and index.
  ISBN 1-56766-459-8 (lib. bdg. : alk. paper)
  1. Gymnastics—Juvenile literature. [1. Gymnastics.] I. Title. II. Series: Wonder books (Chanhassen, MN.)
  GV461.3 .K55 2003
  796.44—dc21   2002015147